5 minute CHRISTMAS STORIES

OM KIDZ

An imprint of Om Books International

Published in 2016

An imprint of Om Books International

Corporate & Editorial Office
A 12, Sector 64, Noida 201 301
Uttar Pradesh, India
Phone: +91 120 477 4100
Email: editorial@ombooks.com
Website: www.ombooksinternational.com

Sales Office
107, Ansari Road, Darya Ganj, New Delhi 110 002, India
Phone: +91 11 4000 9000, 2326 3363, 2326 5303
Fax: +91 11 2327 8091
Email: sales@ombooks.com
Website: www.ombooks.com

Copyright © Om Books International 2016

Content by Swayam Ganguly
Illustrations by Rajeeb Khan, Sijo John Thottam, Shatrughan Kumar

ISBN : 978-93-85252-98-3

Printed in India

10 9 8 7 6 5 4 3 2 1

Contents

The Little Christmas Tree

Once, there lived a little fir tree, who dreamed of being a Christmas tree when he grew up.

"Being a tree with humans is not as good as you think it is," the older, experienced trees advised him, but the little fir tree refused to believe them.

"All I wish for is to be a Christmas tree!" he declared. The little fir tree did not have to wait for long. His wish came true, one snowy day some children arrived with their parents to choose a Christmas tree.

"Oh, Look Papa!" one of the children exclaimed, pointing at the little fir tree. "That one is perfect to decorate our living room."

The other children loved the little fir tree too and the parents agreed to their demand.

The little fir tree was very happy when he was dug up and carried to the living room of the family's house.

'My wish has finally been granted,' the little fir tree thought happily. 'I can now become a real Christmas tree.'

The children adorned their little fir tree with lights and other Christmas decorations. The lights were then switched on and the little fir tree shone bright and beautifully.

"How beautiful I look!" the little fir tree exclaimed proudly when he saw his reflection in the mirror.

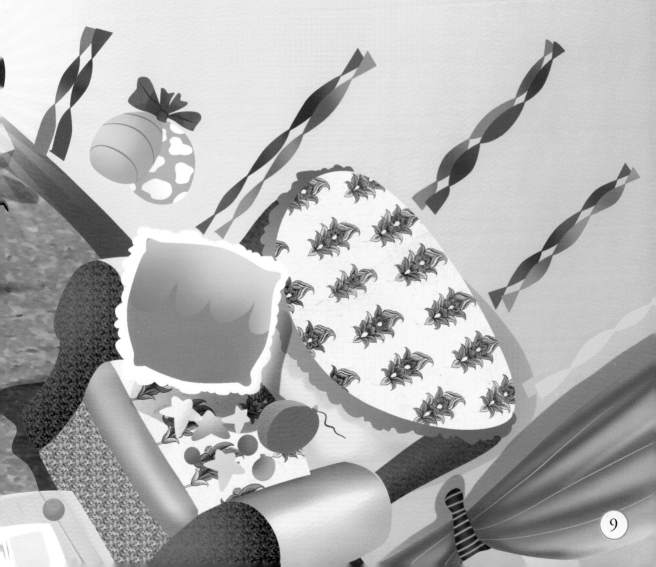

Christmas was fast approaching and all the guests, who visited the house, admired the little fir tree and praised the children for having decorated it so beautifully.

'How wrong the old trees were about people,' the little fir tree thought happily, lifting his branches higher so that everyone could take a better look at him.

The little fir tree was the darling of the family till January.

Then, he began losing his needles and was soon forgotten. No one touched him, looked at him, or even spoke about him.

"Alas!" he exclaimed. "Nobody loves me anymore!"

He was soon locked into the cellar and was very sad that he had been brought here.

After many days, that seemed like many years, the little fir tree was replanted and he was happy again.

He finally understood that he had been locked in the cold cellar so that he could remain healthy.

Every year, the little fir tree was dug up before Christmas and replanted later in the year. 'The old trees were all wrong!' he thought. 'All people are not bad after all!'

Pablo, the Little Polar Bear

Pablo was a small polar bear, who was happiest during Christmas. One Christmas Eve, Pablo asked his mother, "Mom, have I been a good bear this year?"

"Of course, my darling," his mother said to Pablo with a smile.

"Will Santa Claus get me a present?"

"He should," his mother replied.

"May I write him a letter?"

"Yes, dear," his mother said, "but you must go to bed immediately after writing it."

Pablo wrote a letter to Santa Claus, holding the pen with his little paw.

Dear Santa,

I hope you and your little helpers are fine. Mom tells me I've been a good bear and that you shall get me a present this year. I would like to have:

A woolen scarf (it gets chilly here)
A wooden sledge
A fishing rod

It doesn't matter if you cannot get me all the three presents.

Wish you a Merry Christmas,

Love,
Pablo.

'The best gift would be to meet Santa and go for a sleigh ride with him,' he thought.

Then, Pablo fell asleep. He dreamed of an old man with a white beard, carrying a sack full of presents. The old man rode on a sleigh, which travelled faster than the wind.

Pablo woke up in the morning and decided to go to the top of the Snow White Hill, to post his letter. He prepared his backpack that carried his water bottle, lunch and the letter, and waved goodbye to his parents.

It was a long journey and Pablo was so exhausted that he fell asleep on top of the hill. When he woke up, the sun had gone down.

Soon, it started getting darker and Pablo got scared and started crying.

Suddenly, he saw a strange light coming from the sky. Pablo heard the sound of jingling bells, and there he was! Santa Claus had come on his sleigh; pulled by reindeers, he whizzed through the air towards Pablo.

"Santa Claus!" Pablo exclaimed.

"Hop on! Let's go home!" Santa said.

Pablo had the time of his life as they flew in the air on Santa's sleigh. Pablo was so excited that he forgot all about the letter and presents. Nothing else mattered; his wish had come true! The sleigh dropped him home to his worried parents.

"I received the best Christmas gift ever," Pablo exclaimed to his parents.

"So have we, now that you have returned home safe," his mother said and hugged him tight.

Alone on Christmas

Mrs Jones was sad as she had to spend Christmas all alone this year. She was missing her son and her grandchildren, who lived in another city. The city was far away and they could not visit her this year.

'That's really such a shame!' Mrs Jones thought. She would have loved spending Christmas with her grandchildren.

"I think I'll make myself a meal," Mrs Jones decided and the thought made her feel much better. But the wood was wet and the fire just wouldn't light.

"I'll just drink a glass of milk," she decided.

But just when she put the glass of milk on the counter, her cat, Elinor, knocked it over.

"It will be a very lonely Christmas," she said and sat on her rocking chair thinking about the good times.

Christmas had been such a lovely time of the year when her husband had been alive. Friends and family had visited them and the house had been so alive and noisy.

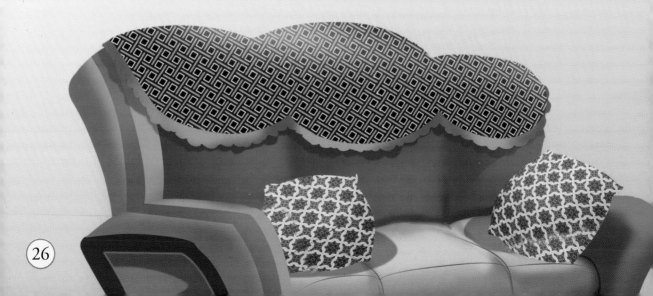

But now, it was so quiet.

Mrs Jones closed her eyes and saw her son and daughter-in-law's face. Then, she imagined her grandchildren's happy faces and smiled.

"Merry Christmas, Elinor," she said to her cat and fell asleep on the chair. Mrs Jones had been asleep for an hour, when she heard some noises. There were people moving around in her house!

Mrs Jones woke up hurriedly, fearing that burglars had entered her home. She could hear someone whispering. 'NO! It couldn't be! It must be a dream!' She closed her eyes again and then opened them as a familiar smell wafted into her nose.

"Why, that smells like turkey and cakes!" Mrs Jones exclaimed. "It smells just like a Christmas dinner!"

She got up from her chair to discover that a cozy fire was crackling in the hearth, the smells were really coming from her own kitchen. The Christmas tree had been decorated and shone with beautiful lights.

"It's too good to be true!" she exclaimed.

"Well, it is true," her son said as he suddenly appeared from behind the door. "Merry Christmas, Mother!"

Her daughter-in-law came out of the kitchen smiling, followed by her grandchildren, who ran into her arms shouting, "Surprise! Merry Christmas!"

It was going to be a merry Christmas indeed for Mrs Jones!

Chubby Cheeks

Chubby Cheeks was a small boy with red, chubby cheeks. He lived in a small house in the mountains, beside a huge forest. Chubby Cheeks would often go for walks to the forest near his house.

Sometimes, a ladybird would perch on his hand and Chubby Cheeks would sing,

Hello ladybird
What a lovely word
You're a bird divine
A lady so fine!

The ladybird would chirp happily and all the trees would swing and shake their branches in approval.

Everyone in the forest loved Chubby Cheeks! Whenever he rested there, the trees sheltered him lovingly and the animals and birds flocked towards him.

One day, Chubby Cheek's parents went to town promising to return on Christmas Eve. But Chubby Cheeks began to get bored.

"Why don't I surprise Mom and Dad by going out to meet them?" he decided.

"Where is Chubby Cheeks going at this time of the evening?" the fir trees said to each other as he entered the forest. Chubby Cheeks waited near the forest path for a long time, but there was no sign of his parents.

Night fell and Chubby Cheeks decided to go back home. But the snow was very thick now and he found it difficult to walk. It became darker and Chubby Cheeks realised that he was lost in the forest. He was scared and cold, and started crying.

"Chubby Cheeks is lost. He's crying," the fir trees whispered to each other. The news travelled to all the birds and animals.

Then, the biggest fir tree picked up Chubby Cheeks and with the help of his neighbour, he made a cozy little hammock for him. The animals too came to his rescue.

Chubby Cheeks was happy to see them and stopped crying. Soon, he fell asleep.

But it was Christmas Eve, and all the trees, birds and animals wanted to give Chubby Cheeks a gift. So they waited for Father Christmas to fly by and told him all about Chubby Cheeks. Father Christmas asked the snow cloud and the Moon for help; they decorated the tallest fir tree.

Then, Father Christmas woke up Chubby Cheeks, who saw the whole forest was lit up for him.

"Wow!" he exclaimed.

"Merry Christmas!" Father Christmas said.

"Merry Christmas!" said the trees, birds and animals.

Nobody believed Chubby Cheeks when he returned home the next day and told his parents the story. But this is exactly what had happened!

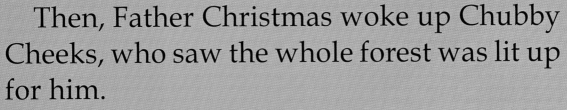

The Christmas Singers

There were three penguins called Robert, Jack and Ben who were great friends. Every Christmas Eve, they sang Christmas carols together for all the animals and birds. But this time, a day before Christmas Eve, Robert took to his bed with a terrible cold.

"Achooo!" Robert sneezed and coughed.

"There's no way Robert can sing if he doesn't get well," Ben said, worriedly.

"Achooo! It looks like you guys will have to sing without me this time," Robert said in a hoarse voice.

"There's no way we'll sing without you, my friend," Ben declared.

"Let's take him to Doctor Coco," Jack suggested and the three friends hobbled over to Doctor Coco's clinic.

"There's only one way to cure Robert in so short a time," Doctor Coco said, after he had examined the patient.

"How?" Ben and Jack asked.

"Achooo!" Robert sneezed.

"The golden seaweed found in the Indian Ocean is the only medicine to cure Robert quickly," Doctor Coco explained.

"Oh no!" Ben wailed. "The Indian Ocean is so far away! There's no way we can get the golden seaweed so quickly."

"I'm afraid we won't have any Christmas carols this year then," Doctor Coco said sadly.

The three friends then started crying on their way home. Their loud sobs were heard by Jerry, one of the smartest ice-fish in the ocean.

"What's the matter?" Jerry asked as he popped his head over the water.

They told him everything.

"Let me see what I can do!" he said. "We must have carols on Christmas Eve."

Jerry dived back into the ocean and sent signals to all his friends. Jerry's distress signal was relayed from the Arctic Ocean to the Pacific Ocean in just a few minutes. Soon, his friends in the Indian Ocean too heard about their dilemma.

The butterfly fish in the Indian Ocean collected the golden seaweed and swam to the Pacific Ocean to hand it over to the starfish who quickly swam to reach the Arctic Ocean, where Jerry and his mates waited.

"There you go mates. That was no trouble," Jerry said as he handed the golden seaweed to the penguins. And it was only noon!

Doctor Coco prepared a strong cup of the golden seaweed herbal tea, which Robert gulped down immediately.

In just a few minutes, he was cured and his voice was back to normal.

The three Christmas singers danced in joy. With his intelligence, Jerry had saved the day.

The Girl with the Matchboxes

It was a cold winter and it was snowing heavily. A little girl walked in the snow with great difficulty. Her legs had turned blue from the cold. The girl was very poor and had no shoes or warm clothes on her.

She shivered in the cold and held a bundle tightly against her chest. It had some matchboxes she was trying to sell. The girl spotted an open window that was well-lit and decided to rest under it for a while.

'I can't return home without selling a single matchbox,' the girl thought. 'Our house is not warm. But let me warm myself by lighting a matchstick,' she decided. The girl lit a stick.

"Ah! it's so warm now!" she exclaimed and drifted into a world of fantasy. She saw herself seated by a huge fireplace.

'Yes! That felt so good,' she thought. But the matchstick went out and the cold returned.

The girl shivered and lit another one and it was warm and comfortable once more.

She now saw a beautiful house. There was a table that was nicely decorated and a freshly-cooked turkey was placed in the middle of it. It was stuffed with apples and other delicacies.

"Oh!" the girl exclaimed. "The turkey has just jumped off the table and is coming towards me now!" The matchstick went out and the little girl lit another one.

This time, she saw a beautiful Christmas tree. The matchstick went out again, but the lights from the Christmas tree didn't, instead she saw them lighting up the whole sky.

"I remember Grandma always said that when a star fell from the sky, it meant that a soul was returning to God!" the little girl exclaimed. "I miss you so much grandma!" the girl sobbed and lit another matchstick.

This time, she saw her grandma, who smiled at her with her arms wide open.

"Don't leave me alone, grandma!" she cried. "Don't disappear when this matchstick goes out. I don't want anything but you!"

The girl lit all the matchsticks at once. There was a great spark of light and her grandmother looked like a fairy.

"I love you, grandma. Please hug me," she pleaded.

The next morning, the townspeople saw the girl lying dead on the snow, but she had a smile on her face. Many burnt matchsticks lay near her. It was Christmas morning.

The Bear and the Trolls

One day, a Norwegian hunter called Stefan trapped a bear cub. He tamed the bear and taught him many tricks. The bear grew up to be a handsome animal.

'I must gift my bear to the King of Denmark,' Stefan thought. ' I am sure he will give me a reward.'

A few days before Christmas, Stefan set off with the bear across Norway. The weather was bad and by Christmas Eve, Stefan had only managed to reach the mountain range of central Norway, known as the Doverfell.

Stefan saw a cottage and decided to rest there for the night. He met the owner of the cottage, a man called Hans, and requested him to give shelter.

"I can't let you stay here," Hans replied. "It's not a safe place to stay. Every Christmas Eve, this place is invaded by a pack of trolls. We sleep in the barn when they come."

Trolls were a band of evil, ugly, fearsome creatures that roamed the countryside and robbed the people.

"We are not afraid of them. Give me a small room in the corner and my bear will sleep near the stove," Stefan requested.

Hans led them inside where a table had been set with Christmas delicacies for the trolls—to keep them happy and stop them from destroying the entire house.

The family went to sleep in the barn. Stefan and the bear slept in the house. The trolls arrived exactly at midnight and were a scary bunch, none of them had any manners. They ate, drank, jumped, danced and broke many things in the house.

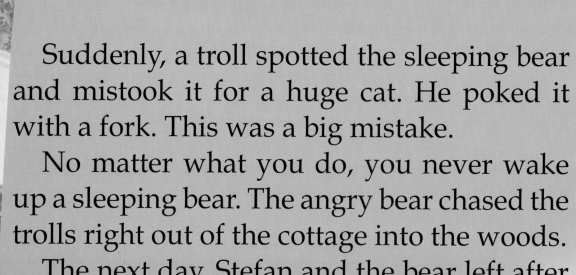

Suddenly, a troll spotted the sleeping bear and mistook it for a huge cat. He poked it with a fork. This was a big mistake.

No matter what you do, you never wake up a sleeping bear. The angry bear chased the trolls right out of the cottage into the woods.

The next day, Stefan and the bear left after telling Hans what had happened. A year later just before Christmas, Hans ran into a troll in the woods.

"Say Hans, is that big cat still with you?" he asked.

"Of course," Hans lied. "She's had five kittens and they are as large and fierce as her!"

"Well, we won't be visiting your house for Christmas again!" the troll declared.

Hans smiled. This was the best Christmas present he and his family could have received.

The Christmas Cherry Tree

When England was ruled by King Pendragon, father of the great King Arthur, there lived a knight called Sir Cleges.

He gifted gold to landowners, offered food to farmers and always helped the poor. The knight's wife, Dame Clarys, was equally kind and noble.

Every year on Christmas eve, Sir Cleges and his wife hosted a grand feast. No guest left empty-handed and Sir Cleges generously donated robes, horses, silver and gold. But this Christmas, so many people had attended the feast that Sir Cleges became penniless after hosting the feast.

On Christmas morning, Sir Cleges prayed before his favourite cherry tree and discovered that it had grown ripe, round cherries.

'How is it that cherries are growing in the winter season?' he thought and tasted one. It was the most juicy and delicious cherry he had ever eaten.

"It must be a gift from Jesus," his wife declared. "We must gift some of these cherries to the King!"

She prepared a basket full of ripe cherries and the poor couple set off for the palace, carrying the basket.

"Do you think the King will meet beggars like you?" the porter said and stopped them at the gates.

"I have a present for the king!" Sir Cleges said and showed him the basket.

"I shall let you pass. But you must promise me one third of whatever reward the King grants you," the greedy porter said.

Sir Cleges agreed.

They were stopped by an usher and a steward after that, and each one demanded one third of the king's reward. Sir Cleges agreed and was finally able to meet the king, who did not recognise Sir Cleges.

"I have brought a basket of cherries for you, my lord!" Sir Cleges said. The King was thrilled when he tasted the cherries.

"Name your reward!" he said happily. "You can have anything you want."

"I want 12 strokes from my stick which I would like to divide between three friends from this castle," Sir Cleges replied. The King was surprised, but granted his request.

Sir Cleges gave four solid blows each to the porter, usher and the steward. The King and his courtiers had a hearty laugh when they heard the whole story.

When the King became aware of his identity, he granted Sir Cleges riches, lands, forests and gold. Sir Cleges and his wife lived happily ever after and continued their Christmas tradition.

TITLES IN THIS SERIES

ISBN:978-93-82607-88-5

ISBN:978-93-82607-76-2

ISBN:978-93-82607-89-2

ISBN:978-93-82607-26-7

ISBN:978-93-82607-87-8

ISBN:978-93-81607-46-6

ISBN:978-93-85252-98-3

ISBN:978-93-85252-97-6